The Miracle Within Me

The Miracle Within Me

by

Angela K Parker

Table of Contents

About The Book

I'D GIVEN MY LIFE to a man who promised to stick by me through thick and thin. I gave up my best friend and the only family I had left to be with him. I moved on and grew into the shell that he molded for me. By the time I realized what I'd done, it was too late. The damage was done. He left me broken and alone. The only good that remained of our broken home is the old pear tree out by the lake and the partridge that often visits me.

On the day my marriage came to an end, Austin found me. He's still everything he once was to me; kind, nurturing, caring, and my best friend. But this time, he wants more. He wants us to be a family. I don't know if I can give him all that he desires. My heart is telling me to take a chance, but what if I'm wrong? What if my past repeats itself, and I'm left alone again to pick up the pieces?

Prologue

Kennedy

I STARE AHEAD in disbelief. I don't understand why this keeps happening to me. This was supposed to be it. I just knew that this time would be different. I did all of the right things. I ate right. I exercised. I prayed.

In the end, none of it mattered.

I'm in shock, just like the last two times. Only this time is much more painful. This time, I've lost so much more.

I search Daniel's eyes for any sign that he might change his mind and reconsider. He stares back at me without an ounce of compassion, his eyes empty and cold. I can't fathom how someone who claims to love me could give me an ultimatum.

Yes. I made a promise, and I did everything that I could to keep it, but in truth, it wasn't up to me. It was beyond my control.

I met Daniel at a job convention during my last year in college. He beckoned me over to his table to see what he had to offer. I don't remember much of what he said that day, but I knew that whatever he had, I wanted. He was charming, handsome, older, and so out of my league. I left his table with a handful of pamphlets and a huge smile. I didn't know until later that he'd slipped me his number. I don't know what made me call him, but I did.

Everything happened so fast after that call. We dated for a couple of months. We both knew what we wanted; the house, the kids, career. We made promises that we would have these things. We would have a family. We were married in the courthouse and got pregnant right away.

Daniel was so supportive when we lost the baby at seven weeks. Six months later, we tried again. Nine weeks into the pregnancy, I had another miscarriage. Daniel wasn't as supportive as the first time. He began to pull away from me. He threatened to leave. I begged him to stay, to give me one more chance to make good on my promise. He agreed.

And here we are, one year later.

Another broken promise.

A shattered marriage with no hope in sight.

Daniel averts his eyes to the doctor as she continues to speak. He's inches away from me, yet we're so far apart.

"There are other options for you to consider. We could run tests to try and figure out the problem. Surrogacy and adoption are also great options."

I turn my attention to her. The full reality of my situation hits me hard as I begin to cry uncontrollably. I've lost everything. There is no time for testing, surrogacy, or adoption because my husband is leaving me. He wants something that I can't give him.

"You don't have to make any decisions right now. Take some time to discuss your options, and when you're ready, let us know." Dr. Hayes focuses on Daniel when she doesn't get a response from me. She gives him a pamphlet that I know all too well. "Try to keep her relaxed for a few days. We have a great doctor here in the hospital if she needs to talk to someone. I'll give you some privacy so she can get dressed."

Daniel doesn't look at me. He doesn't offer any type of comfort when she leaves. He walks to the door and pauses before he turns the knob to leave. He says over his shoulder, "Get dressed. I'll be waiting outside."

He's never been as cold to me as he is at this moment. I know that this time, there will be no reconsideration. He's done, and I'm broken.

Chapter 1

Kennedy

I'VE PROLONGED THE inevitable for as long as I could. For six months, I've been moping around my empty home alone. Aside from the occasional trip to the grocery store, I've only stepped outside to visit my chirping friend on the old pear tree. Nothing good has come from that tree in years, but Holly keeps coming back. She usually takes off for a couple of months, but she decided to stick around this year. I can't say that I mind her being here. She's the best kind of company, the kind that doesn't talk back. She can't tell me that I'm wrong, and even if she does, I don't know it.

Life without Daniel is harder than I thought it would be. He slept on the couch the night we got the news of my miscarriage, and he left the morning after. He filed separation papers that same week. It's been months since I've heard anything at all from him. I've been in an uncomfortable limbo until today. It was the day that I had been dreading, but I knew that it would come.

I never imagined that I would be in this position. I didn't think that I'd be forced to make this decision. I guess somewhere deep inside me, I still hoped that Daniel would come home. Getting a divorce is something that I didn't want to do, but it's what Daniel wants.

Irreconcilable differences. I keep staring at the words in disbelief.

Having divorce papers delivered to my doorstep was a stab straight to my heart. It took me back to the day he walked out on me and never looked back. He doesn't want anything, including me. The house, the land, the car, the money in our joint bank account, it's all mine. He even agreed to pay alimony until the day that I married again. I should be happy that he cared enough to leave me with something, but I'm not. I would give it all up just to have him return to me.

As much as I hate what it means to sign on the dotted line, I know it must be done. The hope of a future fades away with each stroke of my pen. The last letter of my name, our name, marks the finality of our relationship. I don't think that I'll ever recover from this.

Getting dressed was a hard task, but I managed to slip on a black sleeveless dress and a pair of black flats. Our lawyers agreed on an impromptu meeting to settle any differences. I could mail it or call a courier, but I want to see him. I need to see him one last time. I want to look him in his eyes as he rips my heart in two.

When I arrive at his lawyer's office and go inside, I see him. He's as handsome as I remember. He looks happy and focused. I almost smile. I almost go to him until I notice the charm standing a few feet away. She's tall, beautiful, and nothing like me.

My eyes fall closed at the sight of her perfectly round belly. It has to be a mistake. There's no way she could be that pregnant, unless…

I take a deep swallow to fend off the bile in my throat. As much as I wish it weren't, I know it's no mistake when I open my eyes to look at them. Her smile shines brightly for him as he rests his hand on her belly, proving to me that I was the problem all along. He was cheating on me because I couldn't give him what he so desperately desired.

I hold my head high as my lawyer and I walk past them and take a seat at the roundtable. Daniel and his lawyer enter after us, leaving his charm outside the double doors. He sits directly in front of me, tapping his fingernails impatiently against the wood. It takes all of my willpower not to burst into tears while the lawyers take a final look at our signed documents.

What I really want Daniel to do is take his irreconcilable differences and shove them. I want to tear up the papers and take everything he has for what he's done, but that would only make me look like a fool. I won't give him the satisfaction of knowing how much he's hurt me with his actions. It's evident that there is nothing left to salvage. He's made his choice, and I have to learn to live with it. I want this nightmare to be over.

I leave the office when we're done, and I don't look back. It's one of the hardest things I've ever had to do. I walk away from the only man that I've ever loved, leaving him in the arms of another woman, all without a fight. I defy everything that I was taught about marriage so that he could be happy.

I was raised to believe that marriage is sacred, and even when it seems like all hope is gone, do whatever it takes to make it work. Today, seeing Daniel with another woman took what little fight I had left in me. He stopped fighting for us a long time ago.

I stop at the bar on my way home. I've never cared much for this scene, and I'm not a big drinker, but this… the way my life just turned upside down deserves a drink.

The bartender steps into my line of sight when I take a seat at the bar. "Hello, pretty lady. I'm Hank. What can I get you?"

"Vodka and Coke on the rocks, please." I try for a smile that doesn't quite reach my ears.

Hank stares at me for a moment before he responds. "Will you have a ride home, or will I be calling you a cab afterward?" He asks with a small chuckle.

"I haven't decided yet. How about I let you know when the time comes. Deal?" I asked, holding my hand out for him to shake.

He chuckles again. He glances down at my left hand that still houses the ring that Daniel gave me. "Deal, Mrs…" He quirks his brow when his eyes return to mine.

"Ms. Hahn," I correct him. "But call me Kennedy, please."

"Coming right up, Kennedy." He taps the bar and walks away to fetch my drink.

I stare straight ahead at the bottles lining the wall. Nothing around me interests me. Tonight I just want to drink until I'm numb. I give Hank a small smile as he sets my drink in front of me.

"Vodka and Coke on the rocks. Can I get you anything else?"

"No, this will be all for now." I twist the glass on the bar, staring down at the dark substance. It's not something that I would have wanted had things ended differently. This was always Daniel's drink of choice. I thought it fitting that his drink would be the thing that made me forget for a little while.

The first sip burns as it slides down my throat. The sting from this liquid is nothing compared to the burn I feel in my heart. I take another sip and another, and another until my brain begins to fog, until there's nothing left but cold cubes clinking against the glass.

"Hey, Hank! Bartender, can you give me another glass of whatever this is?" I can already feel the effects taking over, but it's not enough. I still remember. I just want to forget. I tap the glass against the bar impatiently.

Hank comes over with a fresh glass half full. I drink it too quickly and ask Hank to bring me another one. Now that I've gotten used to the sting, it only takes me seconds to swallow the third glass.

I slam my hand down on the bar. "Another one, Hank!" I say loudly.

"I think you've had enough, Kennedy." Hank gazes at me with questioning eyes.

I stare daggers at him for wanting to cut me off. Who does he think he is to tell me when I'm done? "I said, an-n-nother one, Hank!" My words slur. I stumble when I try to stand up.

"Whoa." Someone catches me from behind and sits me back down. "Easy," they say, stepping around me.

I see a man standing in front of me through my blurred vision. At first glance, I can't quite make out his face in my drunken state, but there's something about him that's familiar. Or maybe I'm just imagining things.

I grin at the familiar stranger who watches me with keen eyes.

"Kennedy, is that you?"

I jerk away from his strong hands that still hold my arms. "Who are y-you?" I question. "And how do y-you know my n-name?" I stutter.

"It's me, Austin."

Austin. Austin. I try to recall if I know this man or not. Then it finally dawns on me. "Oh! Austin! What are you doing here? You sh-shouldn't be here." I stumble when I try to stand again. Austin's arms wrap around me protectively, holding me upright. I throw my arms around his neck and lean in close to sniff his shirt. "You smell good," I drag out. I tip up and run my nose along the side of his neck to take another whiff of his scent.

"Okay. I think we need to get you home." He pulls my nose off of his neck, continuing to hold my arms. "Do you want me to call Dan…"

"No!" I scream louder than I intend to. "I don't need Daniel's permission for anything anymore. I'm not his responsibility," I say in a calmer tone.

"I'll take you home," Austin says to me. He looks over at Hank. "How much did she have?" He asks.

"Three glasses. Vodka and Coke. I was just about to call her a cab."

"Don't worry about it. I've got her." Austin leans me against the bar and hands Hank his card.

"You don't have to do th-that Austin. I can take c-care of myself." I run my hand across his broad chest.

"Thank you," he says to Hank. He wraps his arms around my waist and guides me toward the exit door. "I know you can, darlin'. You're doin' a fine job, but just for tonight, let's pretend that you can't. Let me take care of you."

"Ha." I chuckle at his statement. *Let me take care of you.* I like the sound of Austin's offer. Daniel has never said those words to me. He's never offered to take care of me. I was always taking care of him. His needs. His wants. His desires. And look where that got me.

Austin stops to say something to a group of guys and hands one of them a set of keys. The evening sun warms my skin when we step outside. A small glare beats against my eyes, causing them to close.

"Where are your keys, darlin'?"

I giggle for no reason at all. "In my p-purse silly." I hand them over and let him guide me to the passenger seat. As soon as I sit down, I lean my head against the headrest and close my eyes, still desperate to forget.

Chapter 2

Austin

I HADN'T SEEN Kennedy in what seemed like forever, but it doesn't matter the length of time between our last encounter. I would recognize her anywhere.

The guys and I were having an early dinner when I heard a young lady shouting at the bar. I never expected that someone to be Kennedy. I didn't expect to have her wrapped in my arms and openly flirting with me. I definitely didn't intend to take her home. Even after all these years, I still can't deny her.

Kennedy and I were the best of friends until she ran off and got married. She forgot about me and everything that we stood for. She found a new best friend and left me behind with nothing but questions. Seeing her tonight like this only adds to the list.

Kennedy fell asleep as soon as her head fell back against the headrest. I didn't like the idea of going through her purse, but it was the only way to know if her address was still the same. I feel bad for allowing her to throw me away so easily. I was her best friend. I should know what's happening in her life.

Kennedy's home is beautiful and huge, two stories high, painted in beige with black shutters. It's just like the home she would always dream about. She doesn't budge when I pull the car into her two-car garage. I'm nervous about bringing another man's wife home, but I don't see Daniel's car anywhere, and I can't just leave her like this.

Stan parks my car in the driveway. Then he brings my keys over and jumps in the car with our other friends. I open the door to her house first, then go back to get her. Her arms hang limply as I pick her up to carry her inside. Her head rests on my shoulder as I close the door behind us.

"Any chance you can tell me where your bedroom is, darlin'?" I ask Kennedy's sleeping form. "No? Guess I'll have to hunt for it."

I look around the large space for direction. There's an open space leading to a dark hallway visible from where I'm standing. I walk in that direction until I find the biggest room. The only room that looks like it's being used.

I breathe her in before I lay her onto her bed. Somewhere underneath the stench of alcohol is a hint of honey. She smells different from what I remember but in a good way. I pull the cover over her and stand there, staring at her expressionless face.

"What happened to you, Kennedy?" I whisper into the quiet room. I've never seen her behave this way. Kennedy is the one who rarely ever took a drink at parties, and when she did, it was never to the point of intoxication. I look around, contemplating whether I should stay or go. I don't want to leave her like this. I need to make sure she's alright.

I go into the bathroom to search her cabinets for pain meds until I find what I'm looking for. I removed two pills from the bottle and set them on her bedside table with a bottle of water. There's a chair in the corner, but being in their bedroom doesn't feel right. So, I go into the living room and sit on the couch.

I think about leaving again, but something keeps telling me to stay. I won't leave her to wonder like she left me years ago. I have to know that she's okay.

I don't know much about her husband, other than his name and him being the reason why Kennedy shied away from me. Hopefully, he's an understanding guy, and when he comes home, he'll give me a chance to explain why I'm here before he blows my head off.

Chapter 3

Kennedy

I TRY TO OPEN my eyes, but my head seems to be running a marathon. I try again and strain my eyes against the morning light. I push myself up into a sitting position on the side of the bed and wince when my feet touch the cold floor. There's a bottle of water and two pills sitting on my nightstand. I don't question how they got there. I take them both and stumble into the bathroom to take a shower.

Ten minutes later, I stumble back into my bedroom, wrapped in my fluffy white robe. I don't remember how I got home last night. I think I remember seeing my old friend last night, but it could've all been a dream in the state I was in. The last coherent thought that I had was asking Hank for another drink.

The walk to the kitchen feels like a mile. Every step trembles inside my head. The pain meds are taking their sweet time providing relief. I stir up some eggs and make a pot of coffee to help the meds along.

I knew there was a reason why I didn't drink so much. Last night I just didn't care, and now… Now I'm paying heavily for it. I can't say that I regret it, though. It served its purpose. It made me forget for just a little while.

I sit my plate of eggs on the table and pour myself a cup of coffee. I stare out into the backyard at nothing in particular with my cup in hand.

"You're lookin' better this morning."

I startle at the voice behind me, and my cup falls to the floor, breaking into pieces.

"Shit! I'm sorry, darlin'. I didn't mean to frighten you."

I turn to find Austin standing in my kitchen.

Austin Reid.

Is in my kitchen. I wasn't dreaming.

"What are you doing here?" Never mind the coffee that splattered everywhere or the broken coffee mug.

He holds his hands up in defense. "I brought you home last night. Don't you remember?" His head tilts to one side, concern etched across his face.

"Well, of course, I remember," I say, lying through my teeth. "But why are you still here?"

Austin's face falls at my question.

"I mean… Not that I mind you being here. Did I… Did we?" My unspoken question lingers in the air, and his eyes widen.

"No. I brought you home and put you to bed. I fell asleep on the couch. Sorry about that. I wanted to make sure you were okay, at least until Daniel came home." He looks around nervously, running his fingers through his hair. "Is he here?"

I look away from him, ashamed to answer that question. How do I tell him that I traded in our friendship for a failed marriage? What will he think of the woman that I've become and me?

"I don't mean to pry. I just thought…."

"It's okay," I tell him, returning my attention to him. "Daniel hasn't been here for a long time. Our divorce was final yesterday."

Sympathy is the last thing I expect to see in his eyes, but it's there. I think I'd much rather he hate me than look at me the way he is.

"Is that what last night was about?"

"Last night was a necessity."

"If I had known, I could've helped you through this. Why didn't you call me?"

I could've called him. The thought crossed my mind a few times, but I had no idea what his situation was or what his life was like now. I was a terrible friend, and I lost touch. My first thought was that I didn't know if the man standing in front of me would've forgiven me or not. I wasn't in the mood for more rejection. But somewhere deep down inside, I knew… I knew that he would be there for me if I needed him, even with how I treated him. That thought was even more terrifying than the last.

"I didn't call because I knew that you would come." I didn't think that I'd be ready to face him until I looked into his hazel eyes.

"Of course, I would've come, darlin'." I can't tell you how many times I've thought about you over the years; how many times I've wanted to call you to catch up."

"I'm sorry for the way I left things, Austin."

"No need to be sorry, Dee."

My heartbeat picks up at the mention of my old familiar name. I haven't been called by that name since the day I left him behind.

"What d'ya say we clean up this mess I caused so we can talk?" He points a finger at the broken glass and spilled coffee across the floor.

"Sounds good." I offer him a smile as we begin cleaning.

Chapter 4

Austin

KENNEDY FIDGETS WITH her hands next to me on the porch swing behind her house. I wonder if she's feelin' what I'm feelin'. Has she ever felt it before? She was my best friend, but I've often wondered what it would be like if we were more.

"So, how have you been, Austin? Do you have anyone special in your life?"

I look at her, shocked that she even cares with everything she's got going on. "I did once upon a time, but things didn't work out the way that I'd hoped," I say, looking her straight in her eyes. I know it's wrong of me to bait her like this, but she's finally free, and I want my Dee back in whatever way she'll have me.

Her mouth parts at my words. Her question sits on the tip of her tongue, but she doesn't ask. She takes a sip of coffee from her cup and places it on the small table next to her.

"Maybe you'll get lucky, and someone better will come along."

"I don't see how that's possible. There's not a day that goes by when I don't think about her. It's been a long time since we talked, but even so, my heart still beats for her."

She looks away shyly.

"What about you? What happened with you and Daniel?"

Her jaw sets and begins to tick. It's a touchy subject, but she needs to talk about it. She needs to get him out of her system, or it'll eat her alive.

"As I said, Daniel and I are divorced now. He left me some months back. He wanted something that I couldn't give him. So I gave him the only thing that I could so that he could be happy. There's no sense in both of us being miserable, right?" She snorts out a laugh. "Besides, when he was here, he wasn't really here, you know? He was just a warm body in a cold marriage with no real future in sight. I was just too blind to see it."

"I didn't know him, but you make him sound like a *great* guy."

She laughs at my sarcasm. I see a glimpse of the girl I used to know shine through. "I used to think so." She takes another sip from her cup. "I gave up everything for him. It was supposed to be him and me against the world until he joined the world and turned against me."

It pains me to see the sad smile on her face. I want to make it better. I want to fix whatever's broken inside of her.

"I wish you had come to me with this sooner." I hold my arms open for her to slide next to me. "Come to papa," I say, attempting to lighten the mood.

"You sure don't look like a papa to me. Wait, are you a papa?" She questions.

"No, but I will be one day if my special someone returns to me."

Her posture slumps at my comment. The sadness becomes more prominent in her eyes. She scoots in close to me, resting her head on my chest. Her fingers run along the chain around my neck.

"Do you ever think about having kids?" I ask.

"That's all I've been thinking about for the past couple of years. It was all that was expected of me, and I couldn't even do that right."

"What d'ya mean, expected of you? Was he forcing you to have a kid?"

Quiet falls over us as I wait for an answer.

"It wasn't like that. We both wanted children, but Daniel…." She pauses, and I hear her sniffle. "Daniel wanted a child so badly, even more than me. I would've tried anything to give him what he wanted, but he gave up. When I miscarried for the third time, he walked away and didn't look back. He was gone long before that, though. I was the one in denial. Seeing him yesterday with his new family proved that. He actually brought a date to our divorce proceedings."

"He did what?" I couldn't have heard her right.

"Oh, that's not the worst part. His date appeared to be on the verge of labor."

"I thought you said that it's only been six months." I look down at the top of her head on my chest, confusion and anger coursing through me.

"As I said, I was the one in denial."

"What an asshole!" I whisper-shout above her head. How could someone treat someone they claim to love that way? Why did she stay and put up with his behavior? I can only imagine the amount of stress she must've been under to have his child. All while he was out screwing some other chick. "Are you alright?"

"I'm coping as best as I can. I've had months alone to think about things."

"What are you gonna do now?"

She raises her head from my chest to look at me. "Now… I live. I've been so focused on what was expected that I forgot to stop and take time for myself. I don't want to think about it anymore. I'm going to let the pieces fall into place on their own and stop trying to force it."

She stands and walks over to lean on the porch, swiping her hand over her cheek.

"Maybe that's been the problem all along," she continues. "I don't know what Daniel's purpose was in my life. Maybe he came along to teach me a lesson."

I walk over and stand beside her. I stare into her tear-stained eyes. "What are the chances that we'd be at the same bar, on the same day, at the same time?" I ask her. "Maybe

I'm meant to be standing here with you at this exact moment for a reason. So you don't have to go through this alone. Don't blame yourself for his shortcomings. He'll regret the day that he let you get away."

She covers my hand with hers. "Thank you, Austin. You're a good guy. How could you stand to be around me after what I did to you?"

"You're my best friend, Dee. No amount of time or distance could ever change that. I admit I was hurt when you cut ties with me, but I understood why you did it. I don't know that any guy would be able to handle the intensity of our friendship. The way we were was like…."

"Magic." She finishes my sentence and smiles.

"Exactly." I wipe the lone tear that slides down her cheek. "And something like that doesn't just disappear, Darlin."

I bring her hand to my lips, lingering for a few seconds before I pull away. I don't care what my day would've been filled with today had I not found her again. Being here with her is all I want to do, for however long she'll let me.

Chapter 5

Kennedy

AUSTIN AND I SPEND the day talking about everything and nothing at all. I haven't felt this good in a long time. I didn't realize how much stress I'd been under and how much I'd missed while under Daniel's thumb.

It's funny how time passed, but nothing seemed to change with Austin and me. He still feels and acts like my best friend. He still calms me like no other person could. At first, I didn't think that it was possible to jump back into something that, not long ago, I thought I didn't need. His being here makes me realize that I need him now more than ever. He's all that I have left in this life.

After my parents passed away, Austin was the only light during my darkest days. I was a fool to give him up and so lucky to have him back.

The small breeze seeping through the screened door barely brushes across my skin. I stand and walk to the door when I hear Holly chirping outside. She's perched on a branch in the center of the almost bare pear tree. I don't know for sure if she's a girl or not, but that's what I'd like to think. Something about her nature seems motherly.

"Is that smile for me?" Austin comes to stand next to me. His arm grazes mine, sending a shiver down my spine.

"It's Holly. She's been acting strange lately."

"Who's Holly?"

I chuckle at Austin's question and nod to the tree outside. "The bird. Can't you hear her? This isn't like her. Her behavior is unusual this year. It's almost as if she's sticking around, waiting for something to happen."

"Are you two good friends? I've always wondered if you'd found someone else to take my place." Austin cocks a brow playfully.

I bump my shoulder into his arm. "No one could ever take your place, Austin. Though Holly has been a great substitute."

"Are you sayin' that you were doin' just fine without me?"

"If you'd call having a bird for a best friend *fine* then, I guess so." I look up, giving him a sad smile. "Seriously though, I don't know how I've survived all this without you. I missed you, Austin. I missed us and the way we were."

"I've missed you too, darlin', but I'm back now." He grabs me by the shoulder and turns me to face him. "We're here. Things are different."

I swallow hard against the look in his eyes. Austin has never looked at me this way before. Even his touch is different. His touch is careful and questioning as he pulls me closer to him. The energy between us has me wondering whether we were always meant to be more than friends. Have I been so blinded all of this time that I didn't notice, or am I reading too much into his gaze?

Austin gently cups my face in his hands while silently asking me for permission. The pressure of his closeness weights my eyes. I tilt my head up to meet his lips.

Kissing Austin is not what I thought it would be. I used to think that kissing my best friend would be the worst thing in the world. It would be awkward. It would ruin our friendship. It would be like kissing the brother I never had, but Austin is no brother of mine. Kissing him feels like the most natural thing that I've ever felt. This chemistry between us could only make our friendship stronger.

My eyes remain closed when he pulls away. I want to store this moment in my memories, just in case Austin wakes up and realizes that he's made a mistake.

His hands settle on my upper arms. "Do you know how long I've wanted to do that, darlin'?"

"How long?"

"Since the first time I ever saw you."

I open my eyes to look at him. I'm confused by his admission. Austin has never shown any interest in me other than wanting to be friends.

"Why didn't you say anything?"

He shrugs. "Being cautious, I guess. I'd seen you turn down guys that approached you, and I didn't want to be just another guy. So, I made a hard choice. I settled for bein' just your friend." His thumb brushes across my cheek. "Not anymore, darlin'. I'm tired of settlin'. I want what so many others couldn't have."

"And you think that I'm that person?"

"I know you are."

"How do you know?"

"Because I love you. I always have, always will."

"What if you're wrong, Austin? What if I'm not the person you think I am?"

He smirks as his arms circle around my back. "If I'm wrong, then I'll learn to love her too."

Without another word, his lips connect with mine, and this time I don't hold back. I let him in. I taste him and feel the urgent smoothness of his tongue sliding against mine. I throw my arms around his neck and allow him to lift me into his arms. I wrap my legs around him, clinging to this moment.

It's been months since my lips have been kissed and even longer since I've been drowned in a man's touch. I want Austin just as bad as he wants me. There's no time for words when we pull apart. I slip out of my panties while he unfastens his pants and lets them fall to the floor. Within seconds Austin has me back in his arms with my dress hiked up and back pressed against the wall.

He peppers my neck with kisses while easing into me ever so slowly. I bite my lip to ward off the tinge of pain before pleasure completely overtakes me.

"Let me see your eyes, Dee. I need to know that you're with me."

The swirl in his eyes entrances me. His movements are all new to me.

"Austin." I acclaim.

I can't believe that my Austin turned out to be such a man. The thought of him claiming me in my living room up against the wall with the door wide open was a forbidden thought until now. The reality of me enjoying him inside of me hurts so good. It hurts to know that I've wasted so much time on someone who didn't love me enough when I had the answer in Austin all along.

"Austin," I say again, wanting more of him, more of this.

"I hear you, darlin'." He answers, curving into me just right and connecting with something inside of me I had no idea was there.

I clamp my ankles around his back as my entire body quakes. Austin continues his movement and lets out a hard grunt, signaling his release.

He steps out of his pants. His eyes hold mine as he walks us into the bathroom. I can barely stand when my feet hit the floor, but Austin is right there to hold me, to clean me up, to let me know that our reckless behavior was not a mistake. It was warranted.

Chapter 6

Austin

SHE SLEEPS LIKE an angel. I'm afraid to move in any direction. I'm afraid that she'll wake up and realize that we made a mistake. To finally have her in my arms after all these years… I don't want to go back to life before her.

From the outside looking in, I had my shit together. The truth is, I was simply existing. My job at the law firm pays the bills, but it's not nearly as satisfying as this. I've never felt this type of connection with any other woman before. They were just a means to an end, but Dee is the means and the end. I know it.

"Are you awake, Austin?"

I smile at the feel of her tickling breath on my chest. "Yeah, I'm awake."

"I think we should talk about last night." She rests her hand on my chest, her finger nervously tapping against my skin.

Here it comes, I think. This is the moment when she politely tells me that I need to leave and that we will never be anything more than friends. I won't give her that chance.

"I'm not sorry about last night, Dee. We're both consenting adults. We both wanted it to happen."

"You're right, which is why we need to talk. I more than wanted you last night, Austin. I needed you. I needed to feel like a woman again, and you made that happen for me, but…."

"There is no *but* Dee. There's just you and me. Nothing else."

"Something like this can ruin a friendship."

"I won't let that happen. If our years apart have taught me anything, it's that friendship isn't easily broken if it's built on a strong foundation. Our foundation is strong, Dee, and I'll cut down anything that gets between the cracks."

She cranes her neck up to look at me. "So, what exactly are you saying?"

I brush away the hair creeping over her eye. "I'm sayin' that I want you. I want everything with you. I don't want to question it. I want to dive in headfirst."

She rewards me with a smile.

"What d'ya say? Do you think you could put up with a guy like me for the rest of your life?"

She pauses to think over my question. Her forehead wrinkles. "But you said you wanted children. I don't know if I could ever give you a child Austin."

"I would love to have a child, but it's not my number one priority. Besides, there's more than one way to do that."

She stays quiet, and I give her some time to think.

"I know you've just gotten out of a marriage. So, take all the time you need. You don't have to answer right now."

"Yes. I don't need to think about it." She blurts out.

"Are you sure?"

"Yes, I'm sure. That wasn't a real marriage. It was a failed arrangement. I never should've let you go."

"You won't regret this," I say, holding her stare. We kiss, sealing our commitment to each other.

Chapter 7

Kennedy

7 Weeks Later

AUSTIN AND I HAD a private ceremony here at the house four weeks after our conversation. His mom and dad were present, along with my only family, Holly, and her new beau, who I've been calling Berry. I'm still not quite sure where Berry came from. He just showed up one day. I assume he's a male. He and Holly get along so well. Now I hear twice the chirping in between the calm.

I could live comfortably for the next few years with what I received in the divorce settlement, but I needed to do something. So, I took a part-time job at a flower shop. Austin insisted that I didn't need to work, saying that he'd take care of everything, but I respectfully declined his offer, and he let it go. I strongly feel that his views about me working are about to change.

I've been in a state of denial for the past week. I can't decide if I'm more excited or frightened. I may be a lot of both. A bead of sweat rolls down my face as I stare ahead at the poster on the wall.

Dr. Hayes enters with a huge smile on her face. "Will Mr. Hahn be joining us today?"

In my fog, I forgot to change my name with the receptionist. "Mr. Hahn and I are divorced. It's actually Reid now."

"Please forgive me. I guess congratulations are in order. Will Mr. Reid be joining us?"

"No. He doesn't know that I'm here." I didn't have the guts to tell him.

"Well, you are definitely pregnant. We need to do an ultrasound to determine how far along you are. Lay back for me."

I lay flat on the table and place my hands by my side while she preps the machine.

"Okay, let's see what we have here."

I don't even flinch at the cold gel hitting my belly. I hear a click every time the probe pauses, and with every pause, my heart beats a little bit faster.

"Do you want to see?" she asks.

Every time I'm asked that question, I foolishly turn my head to look at the monitor, knowing that I'll get attached at the very first glance. This time is no different. My eyes tear up at the peanut-sized embryo that I'll probably never get a chance to meet.

"You're about seven weeks along." She prints a string of pictures and wipes the gel away from me after a few more clicks.

I don't understand how she thinks this is a good thing after the last three times.

"We'll watch you closely, considering your previous medical history. I want to see you once every two weeks for the next two months. If you or Mr. Reid have any questions, don't hesitate to contact us."

"Thank you, Dr. Hayes." I think I'm smiling, but I can't be sure. All I can think about is this baby, how much I want this, and how terrified I am of losing again.

Chapter 8

Austin

I'VE GOTTEN USED TO married life fairly quickly. I assume it's easier with someone I already know so much about. I've traded my afternoons at the bar for precious time with my lovely wife. I like having something to look forward to at the end of the day.

Dee is sitting at the empty kitchen table, staring at a small box when I get home. She doesn't give me her normal greeting. She stays seated and focused on the box between her fingers. Her eyes are brimming with red, a clear sign that she's been crying.

I drop my briefcase and go to her. I pull up a chair next to her, turning her to face me. "What's wrong, Dee. Did something happen?"

She nods and throws her arms around my neck. All I can do is wait while she sobs into the crook of my neck. When her sobs diminish, I pull back to look at her.

"What is it, darlin'? You can tell me anything."

She picks up the box on the table and hands it to me, still unable to speak. I open the lightweight box to find that the inside is much heavier than it looks on the outside. A tiny pair of white baby booties stares back at me. Now I know the reason for her stained eyes, her reluctance to speak, and the nervous tension rolling off of her. Now I know because I feel it too. I feel all of it, but I'm overwhelmed with happiness too.

"Does this mean…?" I swallow hard at the thought of a little Reid running around the house. "We're having a baby?"

She nods slowly and releases a whispered, *"Yes."*

"Yes?" I ask, unbelieving.

She nods again. "But Austin, there's a chance that…."

I pull her to me and cut her off with a deep kiss. I touch my forehead to hers when we pull apart. "We're having a baby."

"Austin." Her breath whisps across my lips.

"Everything in life is a chance, darlin'. Whatever happens, I'm here for it. I'll be here by your side through it all. We're in this together."

I want this baby, but she has to know that I would never turn my back on her for something that's out of her control.

Chapter 9

Kennedy

27 Weeks Later

AUSTIN WAS TRUE to his word. He's been right by my side through it all. The doctor's appointments, morning sickness, late nights when I couldn't sleep; he's been my support. Much to my surprise, he didn't argue with me about continuing to work. He thought it was a good idea to keep my mind preoccupied.

Month three was the hardest for me. I often wondered when something would happen to take our child away from me, all the while hoping and praying that nothing would.

Austin talks to our baby as if he, or she, is on the outside, and baby Reid answers whenever he talks. I admire the bond that they've formed. I'm hesitant to do the same for fear that I'll get too attached only to lose it all. My conversations are kept to a minimum with a *"Hey little one"* or *"How are you doing in there."* That's all I can manage right now until I can finally hold little Reid in my arms.

"Three more weeks and we're in the clear. Can you do that?" I rest my hands on the sides of my belly as I stand on my back porch, enjoying the cold breeze. I smile at the thought of Austin finding me here with no protection from the cold. It's either this or freeze him out of the house. My body can't decide what temperature it wants to be lately.

I gaze out at the old pear tree. Everything about this year has been abnormal. First Holly, then Berry, and now the pear tree that never flourished. It's Christmas eve, and what should be a bare tree is just the opposite. It's standing tall, full of green leaves, and nestled in a bed of snow. Holly and Berry have made themselves a home, and Holly hasn't left the nest in weeks.

I'm just about to go inside when a pair of strong arms wrap around me. I smile and lean my head back against him.

"What are you doin' out here in the middle of the night?" Austin asks. His warmth envelopes me, taking away the cold that I'd soaked up, but I don't mind it at all.

"I couldn't sleep, and I didn't want to wake you."

He places a kiss on my temple, swallowing my hands with his over my belly. "Our little Reid keeping you up again?"

"Yes, but it's okay. I don't mind it. It lets me know that Reid is still…." I get choked up on my last word. *Alive.* I still can't believe we've made it this far. I turn into Austin's chest. "I love the strange and uncomfortable feelings." I tilt my head up to meet his lips.

He kisses me back, ending with a kiss on my forehead. "Let's go inside and get you back to bed."

Austin turns the air up on our way to bed without my asking. I'm always his first concern, even before himself. He's never let on that he was worried about losing this baby. I guess I worry enough for both of us.

*****

I'm awakened by a pain that I've felt too many times before. Instead of panicking, I accept what usually happens next. I tap Austin's sleeping form repeatedly, trying to wake him up.

"Austin, wake up. Something's wrong." I can't help thinking that it's too early. Something isn't right.

"What's wrong, darlin'?"

"Pain. A lot of pain," I say calmly.

Austin jumps into action once my statement registers. He helps me up, grabs my premade bag, and carries me to the car. I don't bother getting dressed. He calls Dr. Hayes on the way to the hospital.

Things happen fast once we arrive at the hospital. I'm rushed into the back to prep for delivery. The nurses move like ants around me, and I follow their words to the letter without realizing it.

I can't believe any of this is actually happening until Dr. Hayes arrives. Seeing her face makes it all real. Seeing her makes it final. Only now does my fog begin to clear.

Dr. Hayes checks the monitors while Austin stands next to me, cheering me on.

"You've got this, darlin'. Someone's anxious to meet you. Everything's gonna be fine."

Hearing the excitement in his voice and the sure look in his eyes calms me. I hold his hand and squeeze when Dr. Hayes says push. My heart nearly stops when she suddenly tells me to stop. Even still, Austin shows no signs of concern.

"You're doing great, darlin'. Just a little while longer."

Austin has always been good at making me believe the unbelievable. This time is no different. He gives me the extra boost that I need to continue when Dr. Hayes says, "One more big push."

I bare down as hard as I can and push. A loud cry echoes through the room. I smile up at Austin, thankful that he's by my side as his face begins to fade away.

Chapter 10

Austin

I WAS WORRIED throughout the entire pregnancy, but I never let Dee see it. I held it together for both of us to keep her from falling completely apart. None of that worry amounts to the terror I feel right now. I can feel Dee's grip on my hand loosen. I see her slipping away from me, and there's nothing I can do to stop it.

I can't lose her. Not now.

I reluctantly let go of her hand and step aside when the Dr. comes over. I hold my breath, waiting for her to return to me, and don't release it until I hear the monitor beeping at a steady pace again.

"She's fine." Dr. Hayes says. "She's just a little tired. Let's give her some time to rest, and she'll be as good as new." She motions in the opposite direction of the room. "Would you like to meet your daughter?"

My heartbeat picks up as I look in that direction. *It's a girl!* We walk over, and I just stare at her for the longest time. When they place her in my arms, all of the worries of the past few months fade away. Having her here with us makes everything worth it. She's premature but already weighs 5.9 lbs. Dr. Hayes says she's very strong and should be able to go home in a week if no problems arise. She definitely inherited my attitude. She refused to wait any longer to be with her mama and came into this world on her own terms.

They only allow me to hold her for a couple of minutes before they take her away to be checked. I'm glad that she's here, and both she and Dee are okay. I'm one proud papa today. This is the best Christmas present that I could imagine.

*****

I lift my head from the recliner when I feel Dee's hand tighten on mine. She's been out for almost an hour, and I've been patiently waiting by her hospital bedside.

"There you are," I say, reaching up to touch her cheek.

She smiles then looks around the room, probably searching for little Reid. We have a few names picked out but haven't decided on one yet.

"The baby?" She tries to sit up too fast and winces.

"Take it easy, darlin'. The baby's fine. They wanted to watch her for a couple of hours before they bring her back."

"It's a girl?" Her hand flies to her mouth as her eyes begin to tear up.

"Yes." I bring her other hand to my lips.

"She certainly made an entrance, didn't she?"

"Just like her mama."

She flinches when she tries to laugh.

The nurse rolls baby Reid inside, and Dee perks up. She seems to forget the pain that she's in as her eyes follow our little bundle.

"Good to see you're awake, Mrs. Reid." She picks the baby up and places her gently into Dee's waiting arms. She goes over the baby's status, asks if we have any questions, and gives her a bottle to feed the baby. "I'll go get Dr. Hayes and give you two some time. If you need anything before she comes in, press the call button."

I join my wife and child on the bed when the nurse leaves the room. "What should we name her?" I ask.

Dee takes her eyes off the baby to look at me, but only for a few seconds. "What do you think about Amani Natalia Reid?"

I put my arms around her and pulled them close to me. I bend to kiss our little angel on her forehead, then my wife on her lips. "I think it's perfect."

This morning couldn't be more perfect.

Chapter 11

Kennedy

I HAVE BEEN IN THE hospital for almost a week, waiting for the day that I could finally take Amani home. I refused to leave here without her. I'd given up on miracles until she was gifted to us. I thought all was lost, that I would never be able to have children of my own. Austin changed everything for the better when he found me again.

Dr. Hayes signs my release forms around the same time that Dr. Newman releases Amani. I sit in the back seat with her on the way home, not able to pull my eyes away for the drive. The ride home is understandably much longer than it took to get to the hospital. My driver is a lot more cautious now that there's a baby on board. Austin glances in the rearview mirror at every stoplight, each time asking, *"What's she doing now."* Each time I giggle and tell him that she's still asleep.

I can't wait to see the finished product of the nursery. We were in the process of getting the baby's room set up before she arrived, but we didn't have a chance to finish it. Austin took a couple of hours every day this week to get it done on his own.

Amani squirms when Austin removes her seat from the car to take her inside. He lays her in her crib, and we both stand there watching her sleep.

"She's beautiful," Austin says, pulling me into his side.

"She is," I reply, snuggling in closer.

"You've had a long week, darlin'." He turns me to face him, taking my hand in his. "We're home. She's safe. Why don't you take some time for yourself? I'll watch her."

As much as I don't want to leave her, Austin is right. I've been running on adrenaline all week. I've barely slept, and now that we're finally home, I can feel my energy diminishing.

"Okay." I relent without a struggle.

I take a quick shower and fall quickly to sleep afterward.

When I wake up, Austin is standing in the nursery window holding Amani. I can't hear what he's saying, but it's cute watching him with her.

"And here's your mommy now." He tilts his head down, placing a chaste kiss on my lips when I step beside them.

"It's nearly dark outside. What are you staring at?"

"I heard a noise, so we came to check it out," Austin says to me. "Didn't we, little angel," he says in a sing-song voice to Amani. "We have more company than when we left." He motions his head toward the old pear tree in the backyard.

I gasp at all the baby Cheepers surrounding the tree. Holly flies up close to the window, stopping inches away. I watch in wonder at the twinkle in her eyes. She peers in at Amani before she returns to her perch. A tear falls from my eye. She's never come this close before. I count it as a good sign that she's welcoming Amani home.

I run a finger across Amani's soft cheek then smile at Austin. I wouldn't have made it this far had it not been for him. He is my angel.

"We have a baby," I say, staring between the both of them.

After everything I've been through, it's still hard to believe that she came from me. Even after all of my doubt, she was determined to survive.

My tiny miracle.

Acknowledgments

Thanks to my family, friends, Parker's Angels, readers, bloggers, and everyone behind the scenes.

Author's Note

Everything that anyone does, big or small, plays a huge part in an author's success. I appreciate you all so very much. Thanks for coming along with me on my journey. If you enjoyed reading my book, please consider posting a review on your preferred site; and don't forget to tell your friends about me.

Until Next Time...

About The Author

59

Angela K. Parker is a country girl with a big heart. She's a South Carolina native with a passion for writing, reading, music, & math. When she's not engaged in any of the above, she's spending time with her family or catching up on the latest movies. She's always had a very active imagination. Now she's putting it to good use.

Connect With the Author

Visit www.angelakparker.com and sign up for Angela's newsletter to be informed of future releases.

Email: angelaparkerauthor@gmail.com

www.ingramcontent.com/pod-product-compliance
Lightning Source LLC
Chambersburg PA
CBHW031422160726
47993CB00003B/1351